Purple Nails
and Puppy Tails

Also by Jill Santopolo

Sparkle Spa
Book 1: All That Glitters

✳ ⁎ ✳ ⁎ ✳ ⁎ ✳

Sparkle Spa

Book 2

Purple Nails and Puppy Tails

JILL SANTOPOLO

Aladdin

NEW YORK LONDON TORONTO SYDNEY NEW DELHI

ALADDIN
An imprint of Simon & Schuster Children's Publishing Division
1230 Avenue of the Americas, New York, NY 10020
First Aladdin paperback edition February 2014
Text copyright © 2014 by Simon & Schuster, Inc.
Cover illustrations and interior spot illustrations copyright © 2014 by Cathi Mingus
Book design by Jeanine Henderson
All rights reserved, including the right of reproduction in whole or in part in any form.
ALADDIN is a trademark of Simon & Schuster, Inc., and related logo is
a registered trademark of Simon & Schuster, Inc.
Also available in an Aladdin hardcover edition.
For information about special discounts for bulk purchases, please contact
Simon & Schuster Special Sales at 1-866-506-1949 or business@simonandschuster.com.
The Simon & Schuster Speakers Bureau can bring authors to your live event. For more
information or to book an event, contact the Simon & Schuster Speakers Bureau
at 1-866-248-3049 or visit our website at www.simonspeakers.com.
The text of this book was set in Adobe Caslon.
Manufactured in the United States of America 0114 OFF
10 9 8 7 6 5 4 3 2 1
Library of Congress Control Number 2013949502
ISBN 978-1-4424-7384-3 (hc)
ISBN 978-1-4424-7383-6 (pbk)
ISBN 978-1-4424-7385-0 (eBook)

For the real Mrs. Franklin—my Gram—

who is strong and sparkly, inside and out.

Special thanks to my glitter-tastic editor, Karen Nagel,

as well as to my super-shimmery writer friends

Marianna Baer, Betsy Bird, and Eliot Schrefer.

Contents

one

Shake It Up Silver

Aly Tanner leaned forward with the Shake It Up Silver brush in her hand. She was about to put the second coat of nail polish on her friend Charlotte Cane's pinkie.

"What do you think?" she asked. "Should Shake It Up Silver be our Color of the Week?"

It was a new idea Aly had—picking a Color of the Week so that everyone who came to the Sparkle Spa would get to know all the nail polish choices one by one.

"I like it," Charlotte said. "Nice and sparkly. My fingers look like little fairy wands."

Aly's younger sister, Brooke, put down the nail file she was using for her best friend Sophie Chu's pedicure. "I need to take a break, Sophie," she said. "Just for a second. This is Very Important Polish Business." Brooke walked over to look at Charlotte's nails.

"Oooh, it's so shiny! I love it, Aly," Brooke said. "Maybe we'll get to paint everyone's nails with silver glitter."

"Silver glitter? Let me see," Jenica Posner called from the sitting area. Jenica was the captain of the Auden Elementary girls' soccer team. She already had a special rainbow sparkle soccer team pedicure, which Aly had done three days ago.

Aly topped Charlotte's nails with clear polish to seal in the sparkles and sent her over to the waiting area to dry—and to show Jenica the color.

"Can you give me a quick manicure too, Aly?" Jenica asked after seeing Charlotte's nails. "Before my nana's done out there?"

Aly smiled to herself. She couldn't believe that Jenica Posner, the most popular sixth grader in their school, was begging *her* for a manicure.

Just a few weeks ago Aly and Brooke had given Jenica a rainbow sparkle pedicure, which was how the Sparkle Spa began in the first place. In her next soccer game Jenica scored five goals, and then the rest of the team wanted matching pedicures for good luck. It was pretty unbelievable, but ever since they started getting rainbow pedicures, the team hadn't lost one game. Now Jenica liked to visit and would stop in whenever her grandmother came to True Colors to get her nails done.

The Sparkle Spa was really just a back room of Aly

and Brooke's mom's nail salon. The sisters had opened it and decorated it with paintings and rainbow-colored pillows to sit on. There were some old pedicure chairs and manicure stations for them to use. And the best part was that their mom let them polish kids' nails there three days a week—two days after school and one day on the weekend.

Aly opened the door and looked into the True Colors salon, where all the grown-ups were having their nails done. It was Friday afternoon, *always* a busy time.

Joan—Aly and Brooke's favorite True Colors manicurist—was taking polish off Jenica's nana's nails. Aly figured she could do a manicure almost as fast as Joan could, so the timing might work out perfectly. She waved to Mrs. Franklin, a True Colors regular who had a tiny dog named Sadie that she sometimes brought to the salon with her. Sadie was sitting on Mrs. Franklin's lap, so Aly waved to her, too. Then she slipped back into the Sparkle Spa.

"Sure," Aly told Jenica. "I can do it."

As Aly started on Jenica and Brooke finished up Sophie, Lily Myers walked in the door. Lily was Aly's best school friend, along with Charlotte.

"Hey, guys," Lily said as she climbed into the second pedicure chair, next to Sophie. "Can someone do my toes?"

Brooke looked at Aly with a Secret Sister Eye Message that involved scrunched-up eyebrows. It meant: *Our friends need to start making appointments!* But she leaned over anyway and turned on the water in a pedicure basin for Lily.

"I'm almost done with Sophie. Then it's your turn," Brooke said. "Did you pick a color? If not, I think you might like Shake It Up Silver. It's on Charlotte's nails if you want to see. It's our Color of the Week."

It seemed like Brooke never stopped chattering. She could paint nails and talk, run water and talk, chew gum and talk—Aly was surprised she didn't talk in her sleep.

"Color of the Week?" Lily popped out of the pedicure chair to check out Charlotte's nails. But before she could take even one step, a barking and yapping ball of fur came racing through the door and ran right into Lily's legs.

Lily jumped up and toppled into the almost-full pedicure basin. The water splashed all over Brooke. And the yapping ball of fur—which was actually Mrs. Franklin's dog, Sadie—kept barking and running around the Sparkle Spa.

Jenica hopped up from the manicure chair to chase Sadie, waving her wet Shake It Up Silver nails. "Stop! Sit! Stay! Down! Heel!" she yelled.

"Help!" Lily shouted. She was stuck, sitting in the

pedicure basin, her knees folded up to her chest.

But Sadie wasn't paying attention to either girl. She darted by Aly's feet. Aly dove after her, but the dog got away. Then Sadie headed to the jewelry area and—bam!—knocked over an open box of beads.

"Don't let her eat those!" Jenica said, still running after Sadie.

Charlotte tried to grab Sadie with her elbows so she wouldn't mess up her manicure, but Sadie was faster and raced toward the table with the Sparkle Spa donation jar on it.

Brooke wiped her wet glasses on a dry part of her shirt and scooted across the room, catching the big teal, strawberry-shaped jar just before it fell.

"Help!" Lily yelled again. "I'm stuck!"

Sophie swung her legs back and forth, yelling, "Get her! Get her!"

Aly cornered Sadie between the mini-fridge and a stack of nail polish boxes, bent down, and swooped the panting dog into her arms.

Sadie squirmed and squiggled, but Aly wouldn't let her go. She tried to calm the dog by stroking her head, but Sadie just yapped and yipped and started whimpering.

Mrs. Franklin burst into the Sparkle Spa, with Jamie, the manicurist who usually did Mrs. Franklin's nails, behind her.

"Oh no," Mrs. Franklin said. "Oh dear."

Aly looked around. The place was a mess!

Pedicure water was everywhere. Bottles of Key Lime Pie, Reddy or Not, and Go for the Gold were all over the floor. Lily was still stuck in the pedicure basin, and multicolored beads were rolling across the carpet from the jewelry-making area.

"I don't know what got into her," Mrs. Franklin said, hurrying over to Aly to take the shaking Sadie from her. "A truck horn blared on Main Street, and she took off like a shot."

While Mrs. Franklin soothed Sadie, Jamie pulled Lily out of the pedicure basin. Brooke handed her a few washcloths from a pile she had grabbed to help dry her off.

"I think I need some new clothes," Lily said, trying to blot her shorts dry.

"I have an extra pair of soccer shorts in my duffel," Jenica volunteered, and went over to the couch to get her bag.

"Sadie girl," Mrs. Franklin said, shaking her head at the dog. "Just look at you! What are we going to do now?"

"She'll dry pretty soon," Brooke said. "Or do you

want some washcloths? They're kind of small, but they're probably about the right size for Sadie."

Mrs. Franklin shook her head again. "It's not that," she said. "Sadie was just groomed this morning. She has a dog-modeling job tomorrow at three o'clock. She's the new spokes-dog for the shelter on Taft Street, Paws for Love. They're planning to photograph her for a poster to promote pet adoption. And she's a mess! I'm even going to have to clean her toenails."

Sadie was finally quiet, happy to be in Mrs. Franklin's arms. It was funny how they kind of looked alike. They both had fluffy hair that was mostly white, and Sadie's red collar matched the red sweater Mrs. Franklin had draped over her shoulders.

"Hey, that's the shelter I volunteer at," Jenica said, still rifling through her duffel bag for shorts. "I didn't realize Sadie was the dog that was going to be on the Adoption Day posters."

"Mrs. Franklin? Are dog toenails like people toenails?" Brooke asked. She dropped the wet towels she was holding into the basin and walked over to inspect Sadie. Aly followed her. She'd never really looked closely at a dog's toenails before either.

Mrs. Franklin held up Sadie's paw. "Here they are," she said. "Different from ours."

Brooke took Sadie's paw in her hand. And then she looked at Aly. She was wearing a face that said: *I have an idea!*

"Do you think . . . ," Brooke began. "Do you think we could give Sadie a pedicure tomorrow?" Then she started laughing. "Not a pedicure . . . a pet-icure! Get it?"

Aly got it, and she giggled for a second too. But

then she stopped. She wasn't sure this was the best idea Brooke had ever had. Brooke had lots of ideas all the time. Some were really good, like the name Sparkle Spa. But a puppy pedicure? That sounded like trouble.

two

Purple Paws

Aly bit her lip. She looked at the mess around her. "I, um, I think we have to talk this over, Brooke," she said. "We've never even done a pet-icure."

From her perch on the pedicure chair, Sophie said, "I'll help!"

"Me too!" said Charlotte.

"And me," said Lily, who was behind a closet door, changing into Jenica's shorts.

"I wish I could," Jenica said. "But we have a soccer game."

Aly knew they would have to check with Mom first, but she figured that five of them would hopefully be enough to handle Sadie.

Mrs. Franklin smiled. "Thank you, girls. I'm—or rather, Sadie is—willing to give it a try. Why don't you ask your mother and let me know. Here's my phone number," said Mrs. Franklin, handing them a business card with Sadie's picture on it. "Now say good-bye, Sadie."

Sadie wagged her tail and yipped twice.

Mrs. Franklin, Sadie, and Jamie returned to True Colors. "Would you still like your manicure?" Jamie asked as they walked out the door.

Mrs. Franklin looked down at her nails and sighed. "I think I'll reschedule for early next week and come *without* Sadie."

Aly thought that was a very good idea. Maybe there should be a rule about no pets in the salon. In fact, Aly was surprised her mother hadn't come up with that rule already, since Mom was kind of the queen of rules—there was even a No Dogs Allowed rule in their house. Would she make a rule about pet-icures?

Aly woke up Saturday morning with a knot in her stomach. She couldn't believe Mom had actually said yes to Sadie's pet-icure, that "one little dog, one time, would be fine."

Brooke, still asleep, rolled over in her bed across the room. She squeezed her stuffed monkey, George.

Aly loved Brooke—more than anyone else on the planet, really—but lately it seemed like Brooke was coming up with one crazy plan after another, and then it was Aly's job to make sure that they didn't turn into total disasters.

There was Heather Davis's birthday party, which

Brooke agreed to before the Sparkle Spa was even open for business. And then there was last week's fiasco, when Brooke added Red-Hot Pepper polish to the hand lotion so it would turn pink. The problem was that it also turned people's hands pink. And their arms. And feet, too. It took a lot of polish remover to get their skin back to normal.

The best way Aly knew to try to avoid disasters was to prepare herself as much as possible. So she got up super quietly from her bed and tiptoed over to her desk. She pulled out a piece of paper and a sparkly gel pen—her favorite kind—and started a list:

Perfect Pet-icure Rules
1. No running in Sparkle Spa (people or dogs)
2. No fur polishing (people)
3. No biting (dogs)
4. No chewing chairs, pillows, flip-flops (dogs)

Aly chewed on the cap of the pen. Writing the list had made her a little less worried. As long as she had a plan, she was pretty sure she could handle anything. Even polishing a puppy's nails.

A few hours later Aly and Brooke were in True Colors with their mom. Luckily, they didn't have any appointments at the Sparkle Spa until eleven o'clock, so they'd told Mrs. Franklin to bring Sadie early.

"Girls," Mom said, "please be extra, extra careful today. I don't want either of you to get hurt, and I don't want the back room destroyed."

"We will," Brooke said. "We promise. We'll be the carefullest we've ever been."

Aly nodded. "Charlotte, Lily, and Sophie are coming to help. Plus Mrs. Franklin. Sadie won't be able to run around. We'll make sure she behaves."

The front door jangled, and in walked Miss Lulu,

one of the salon regulars. Every Saturday at 9:30 on the dot, she got a pedicure. But for the past two weeks she'd been away on her honeymoon.

"You're back!" Brooke screeched. "Do you have pictures? What color dresses did the flower girls wear? How was Maine? Did you see a moose?" Brooke ran over to Miss Lulu and hugged her.

Mom took her seat at pedicure station number one, tucking a strand of hair behind her ear. "Slow down, Brooke," she said with a laugh. "I have to do Lulu's toes. You can visit with her while she's drying."

Brooke gave Miss Lulu a final hug and then headed to the Sparkle Spa with Aly. As they opened the door, Mom called, "Remember what I said. I don't want any surprises next time I come back there!"

✳ ✳ ✳ ✳ ✳

But from the minute Mrs. Franklin and Sadie showed up, it was one surprise after another.

First, Mrs. Franklin was late. She came rushing into the spa with Sadie, a little bit out of breath. Sadie had purple bows clipped on top of her ears with rhinestones in the center of each bow. She was also brushed and washed and much fluffier than she'd looked yesterday.

"She's sooo cute!" Sophie said, running over to pet her.

"Do you think I can get bows like that for Minerva?" Charlotte asked. Minerva was Charlotte's poodle and was also the cuddliest dog Aly had ever met. She loved going to Charlotte's house so she could squeeze in as many puppy cuddles as possible.

Back in first grade, when she first started playing with Charlotte and Minerva, Aly asked if the

Tanners could get a dog, but Mom and Dad had said no. That was when the No Dogs Allowed rule was established, and it had been a rule at the Tanner house ever since.

The second surprise was that a man with a camera rushed into the salon after Mrs. Franklin.

"Great news, girls!" Mrs. Franklin said. "Isaac's the photographer who's doing Sadie's photo shoot later. He wanted to take pictures of her getting ready so that Paws for Love can post an Internet feature. Isn't that wonderful?"

Aly started to panic. Wait a minute. This wasn't part of the plan! *They* were going to be in a photo shoot too? Aly checked to make sure she didn't have any nail polish on her clothes. Brooke straightened her glasses. And Charlotte said, "I'm so glad I had my nails done yesterday!"

Aly looked at her own fingers. No polish. She kind

of wished she had time to do her own nails before the photo shoot like she and Brooke did on Saturdays. Or that she was wearing a different shirt—her favorite one with the purple and green stripes.

Finally, Mrs. Franklin handed Aly two tubes filled with Purple Paws puppy polish. It wasn't what Aly expected—the polish wasn't in a bottle like people polish—it looked more like a marker, the kind Aly drew with in art.

Aly uncapped one tube and tried it on her own left thumb just to check it out. It dried in about two seconds.

"You should need only one coat for Sadie's nails," Mrs. Franklin said. "Or at least that's what Nina at the pet store told me." Mrs. Franklin handed Sadie to Brooke, who took her to the area they had set up for the pet-icure. Aly followed. She figured they could trust Miss Nina and her polish information because she was a True Colors regular too.

Sophie sat down, and Brooke put Sadie in her lap.

Charlotte held on tight to her leash.

Lily stood nearby with a just-in-case doggie treat.

Isaac took what seemed like a gazillion photographs.

And Sadie was happy as could be, soaking up all the attention.

Aly pushed the fur out of her way so she could see Sadie's nails better. They were skinny and black and kind of long. The purple color was bright and sparkly, and Miss Nina was definitely right: no second coat needed. It was actually almost easier than doing a pedicure on some people Aly knew—especially ticklish ones.

"This is usually what Sadie's like," Mrs. Franklin said. "It's why the shelter chose her for the Adoption Day campaign."

"What is that about, anyway?" Brooke asked. While she was waiting for her turn to polish Sadie's back nails, Brooke was busy making a string of beads—purple, silver, and pink—to wrap around Sadie's collar.

"The shelter is trying to get the ten dogs that have been there the longest adopted," Mrs. Franklin explained. "And they think that with an adorable spokes-dog like Sadie, people will come running to the shelter. These puppies really need homes, girls. If you met the dogs, you'd understand."

Aly finished Sadie's left paw just as Brooke finished beading. She sat next to Sadie, took the "paw-lish" from Aly, and started painting.

Sadie's tail was wagging so hard, Brooke almost got a splotch of paw-lish on Sadie's fur.

"Stop moving!" Brooke laughed. "You'll ruin your pet-icure!"

Lily gave Sadie her treat and then said, "Maybe we can visit the shelter tomorrow. My brother's allergic, but, Charlotte, maybe you could adopt another dog to be friends with Minerva."

"Maybe," Charlotte said. "Sometimes I worry that she gets lonely when Caleb and I are at school."

"That's such a great idea," Brooke said. "Can we go too?"

Aly nodded. "We're open today, so closed tomorrow. Let's do it."

"That would be lovely, ladies," Mrs. Franklin said. "And thank you all so much for making Sadie a star."

Just before they left, Isaac had Aly, Brooke, Sophie, Lily, and Charlotte pose around Sadie for one last photo. "Say 'puppies'!" he said.

All the girls said "PUPPIES"—Brooke the loudest.

What a fun morning! Aly thought. But now she

and Brooke had to get ready for some human customers. Two new girls from school—twins—who had asked for matching Blueberry Blue birthday pedicures. Aly hoped the two-legged customers were as well-behaved as the four-legged one!

three

Tickled Pink

I s it just me, or does this place smell a little?" Lily asked the next day, when Aly, Brooke, Lily, Charlotte, and Sophie were dropped off at Paws for Love.

Brooke sniffed loudly.

"Ewww. It does smell," Brooke said.

Aly looked around, trying to figure out where they should go, when she saw a very familiar ponytail.

"Jenica?" she said.

Jenica put a bag of dog food she was carrying down on the tile floor. "Hi," she said. "What are you all doing here? How did Sadie's pedicure go?"

"The pet-icure," Brooke corrected her. "And it was awesome!"

Jenica raised an eyebrow.

"It was," Aly said. "Sadie was really well-behaved. And Mrs. Franklin told us all about Adoption Day. She said we should come meet the dogs that need to get adopted."

Jenica picked up the bag of dog food again. "Come with me. I was just bringing this food over to that part of the shelter. Are you guys thinking of adopting a dog?"

"Maybe," Brooke said.

Aly shot her a look. "We're not allowed," Aly said. "But Charlotte might."

"If I can get my parents to agree that two dogs are better than one," Charlotte added. "I mean, *I* think that's true."

"Me too," Jenica said. "I have two dogs. And two cats—all from here."

"I wish I could have that many pets," Sophie said. "All I have is a gerbil."

Jenica dropped off the dog food and led the girls into a room with ten cages. "These are our old-timers," she said. "They're not really old, but they've been here so long we gave them temporary shelter names. They all answer to them now."

Brooke raced over to a cage with a sign that said MELVIN. Inside was a super-slobbery-looking dog.

"Look at this one," she said. "Hi, Melvin. Don't you wish we could have him, Aly?"

Aly looked at the dog. He had soft brown eyes and a wagging tail, but his slobber would be everywhere! No wonder he was an old-timer. She didn't want him.

Then Aly spotted a teeny-tiny dog curled up in the back corner of a cage. He was all eyes and ears with a curly little tail, and he was shaking. Shivering, really. The sign on his cage read SPARKY. He was the cutest dog Aly had ever seen. And clearly, he needed someone to love him.

"Actually," Aly said, "this is the one I wish we could have." She kneeled down next to Sparky's cage and put her fingertips near the bars. Sparky sniffed her fingers with the tiniest nose ever—one that was cold and just a tiny bit wet—and then licked the tip of Aly's pinkie. Aly melted. How could she leave this dog here? She hated the No Dogs Allowed rule more than ever!

"That one?" Brooke made a face. "He looks like a rat."

"A what?" Aly wanted to yell at Brooke, but instead all she said was, "I think he's cute."

And for the rest of the shelter visit, Aly ignored Brooke. She ignored her while they met the other old-timers: Laces and Sneaker and Bob and Murphy and Reginald and Penny and Marjorie and Frida. She even ignored Brooke when she started telling Sophie how she was going to get her mom to change the rule so they could adopt Melvin. Aly knew the rule couldn't be changed. And she knew that even if it could, Mom would never agree to disgusting, slobbery Melvin.

Jenica came into the room with a tall lady who had long braids with beads on the ends that clicked together when she moved. "Everyone, this is Irena. I told her you were the ones who painted Sadie's nails, and she wanted me to introduce her to you."

"It's so nice to meet you girls," Irena said. "Sadie looked beautiful with her nails polished."

"I loved her bows, too," Charlotte said.

"Me too." Irena looked at the cages around her. "It's too bad these puppies can't all get pampered like

Sadie. It might improve their chances of finding a home."

Aly looked around the room. Irena was right. These dogs really could use some spiffing up.

"Ah, well," Irena continued. "Let's hope the Adoption Day campaign will bring in so many people that each dog will find its perfect match."

Aly hoped so. She really hoped so for Sparky. He needed an owner to love him. Aly kind of thought he needed *her* to love him, but that wasn't even worth thinking about. She looked at her purple polka-dot watch. Almost two o'clock. Time to head back to True Colors for the weekly Sunday Pizza Picnic with Joan.

"That would be great," Aly told Irena. "It was really nice to meet you and the dogs."

"Especially Melvin," Brooke said. "I love Melvin."

Irena's eyes lit up. "Would you like to adopt him?"

Before Brooke could answer, Aly said, "Our parents won't let us have a dog. Even though we wish they would."

"I'm going to talk to my parents about this one, though," Charlotte said, pointing to Bob, a black poodle. "I think he and my dog Minerva might get along. She's a poodle too, but a brown one."

"Bob is a sweetheart. I'll keep my fingers crossed," Irena said.

As the girls made their way back through the shelter, they ran into Miss Nina, Mrs. Franklin, and Isaac, who were choosing which pictures of Sadie to use for the Adoption Day advertising.

Aly never thought that today would end with *both* sisters wanting to adopt old-timers. It turned out there were a lot of nice surprises in a smelly shelter.

four

Up the Lavender to the Roof

On Tuesday, after school, Brooke and Aly were in the Sparkle Spa, finishing up their homework—Sparkle Spa Rule Number 1—before opening for business.

Brooke hadn't mentioned Melvin all day, so Aly didn't say anything about Sparky. Aly hated being mad at her sister, and she figured that as long as they didn't talk about dogs, she wouldn't have to be. But that didn't mean she'd stopped thinking about shelter pups, especially Sparky. It made it kind of hard to concentrate on homework.

"Aly?" Brooke asked, looking up from her worksheet. "Did you have to do decimals in third grade?"

Aly stuck her finger on the word "secret" in her copy of *Bridge to Terabithia* to save her place. Chapter four was her fifth-grade assigned reading homework, and she was almost finished.

"Everyone at Auden Elementary has to do decimals in third grade," she said. "How come?"

Brooke pushed her glasses up to the top of her nose. "Decimals go with money, right? That's how you add up all the donations in our jar?"

Aly nodded. "Uh-huh. We studied money in third grade too. Like, how many nickels are in a dollar and all that. . . . The answer is twenty, in case you're wondering."

"How many nickels are in ten dollars?" Brooke asked.

Aly looked down at her finger, which was still resting on the word "secret." Then she looked at her watch. "How about I tell you after we finish our homework? We need to open the Sparkle Spa in five minutes—Tuesday is Soccer Team Rainbow Pedicure Day."

"Oops," said Brooke, looking back at her worksheet. "I forgot. I'd better finish this math sheet."

Aly closed her eyes for a long second and opened them again. Sometimes it seemed like there were so many ideas whirling around in Brooke's brain that she forgot regular stuff that had to happen. But today she really couldn't blame her sister. She wondered if Brooke was thinking about the shelter dogs too.

A few minutes later, just when the girls had finished their homework and started setting up for the soccer team's pedicures, Joan stuck her head into the Sparkle Spa.

"Joanie Macaroni!" Brooke said, smiling. "You weren't here when we came in after school."

"Brookie Cookie!" Joan laughed. "I was delivering brownies for a party tonight at the Paws for Love animal shelter."

Aly finished the last word of chapter four and looked up. Joan was the best baker she and Brooke knew. Sometimes Joan baked cookies and brownies for special events like birthday parties and anniversaries. But Joan baking brownies for the Paws for Love was something new. "That's the same shelter that Sadie's the spokes-dog for!" Aly said.

"I know," Joan said. "It's all Mrs. Franklin has been talking about." She handed Aly a small plastic bag with two brownies inside. "Here's one for each of you. I have to do Mrs. Howard's nails now. See you both later."

By the time Joan was out the door, Brooke was

already standing next to Aly, waiting for her brownie.

"This is soooo good," Brooke said after she swallowed her first bite. "It's really chocolatey, but I think there's also something a little salty in there."

"And maybe some caramel? I like the crunch." Aly examined the size of the brownie. "It could be a little bigger, though."

"Do you think people would pay money for Joan's brownies?" Brooke asked through her second mouthful.

Aly swallowed. "They already do," she told her sister. "I bet Paws for Love paid a lot to have her brownies at their party."

Brooke shook her head. "I mean regular people. What if Joan made brownies and we sold them in True Colors? Then maybe we could give the money to Paws for Love to get bows and pretty collars for the old-timer dogs."

Aly stopped mid-chew. She didn't want to talk

about dogs with Brooke, but this was an awesome idea. "I wonder . . . ," Aly said. "I wonder if Joan can make cookies for dogs, too, and their owners could buy them. And maybe if we raise enough money, we could get puppy polish and give all the dogs pedi-cures."

"You mean 'paw-lish' and 'pet-icures,'" Brooke said with a smile. "Awesome!"

"Hi, guys."

The sisters turned around. They'd been so excited that they hadn't noticed that Jenica and Bethany, the first two soccer players with appointments, had arrived.

"What's up?" Jenica asked. She and Bethany climbed up into the pedicure chairs and Aly filled them in. Brooke interrupted every five seconds with "It was my idea."

Aly would have to tell Brooke later that it wasn't

really polite to brag. "We also thought we could give them all pet-icures," she said.

"I love that idea!" Jenica said. "The dogs need baths, too."

"And maybe little sweaters," Bethany added. "I mean, if you want them to look their best, they need cute outfits."

Brooke clapped her hands. "They totally need outfits!"

Aly thought about bows and outfits and fancy new collars, maybe even bandanas for the boy dogs, then all the paw-lish they'd need for ten dogs. "I'm not sure if Joan's brownies or doggie treats will make us enough money for all that," she said.

Brooke ran over to the sparkly teal strawberry that served as the Sparkle Spa's donation jar and lifted it up. "We can donate all the money that people give us for polishing nails," she said.

Aly was pretty certain it still wouldn't be enough.

"What else can we do to make money?" Jenica asked as Aly polished her pinkie with Under Watermelon.

Aly asked, "What else are we good at?"

Bethany thought for a minute and said, "We can wash cars. Or walk dogs. I can feed my neighbor Mrs. Berman's cat."

Brooke was starting on Bethany's right foot when she said, "We're good at polishing nails."

Aly stopped Jenica's pedicure in the middle of her big toe. That was it! A polish-a-thon!

"Remember when we did that math-a-thon at school?" she said, and started to polish again. Auden had held an event where people donated money for every math problem the students finished, and then all the funds were given to a hospital that treated kids with cancer.

"Sure," Jenica said.

"Well, what if we had a polish-a-thon and people donated money each time we polished someone's nails?"

"You can do that, but wouldn't it be easier if you just asked for a donation from the person who was getting their nails done instead?" Bethany asked.

That was a lot like charging money, it seemed to Aly, and Mom had said no charges for Sparkle Spa services. Just donations. But maybe this would be different, if it was just for one day.

Aly knew she'd have to compose a list to convince Mom. She'd come up with the list later. Right now they had the rest of the soccer team to do.

But then Bethany said, "I've been thinking about a manicure, too. But maybe not the same one Jenica has."

"Hey! I like my color," Jenica said.

Bethany shrugged. "It's nice, but I want something different."

Brooke jumped up. "I know—Up the Lavender to the Roof." She ran over to the polish display and pulled down a bottle of a really light lavender shade, with dark lavender sparkles. "Cool, right?" she said, handing it to Bethany.

"Actually, it *is* pretty awesome. Can you do it?"

Aly looked at her purple polka-dot watch again. Adding this manicure would mess up their schedule a bit, but if she finished up Jenica's toes especially quickly and then started on Bethany's hands while Brooke was finishing up her feet, it just might work.

"Okay. We can do it," she said.

Jenica leaned back in her pedicure chair and pressed the little button that activated the back massage built into the chair. Bethany did the same. "So, do you think Woodrow Wilson is going to be a tough school to beat?" Bethany asked Jenica.

Jenica shrugged. "As long as Maxie and Joelle keep assisting each other up near the goal, I think we can handle it. Plus, remember, we have sparkle power," she said, wiggling her toes.

"What do you think?" Aly began. "Would the soccer team and their sparkle power want to help out if we get my mom to agree to the polish-a-thon?"

"Let's find out when the rest of the team gets here," Jenica said.

Just then Brooke and Aly's mom came into the Sparkle Spa to refill the mini-fridge with water. "Find out what?" she asked.

Aly sighed. She wasn't ready to ask Mom about the polish-a-thon. But Brooke started talking immediately.

"We want to hold a bake sale and polish-a-thon

to raise money for Paws for Love," she said. And then she blurted out the whole plan. It wasn't the way Aly would have explained it, but Brooke got the point across.

When Brooke finished, Aly held her breath.

Mom pressed her lips together for a second. It was one of the things she did when she was trying to make a decision. She loaded the mini-fridge and didn't say anything for a while. "You know," she finally said, "I think that would be great for True Colors to do too. Why don't we have a polish-a-thon for kids in the Sparkle Spa and one for adults in True Colors? Then we'd raise even more money, and maybe get newspaper coverage too.

"We can put flyers up all over town. It would give us a leg up over that Princess Polish shop that's supposed to open across the street next month." Mom barely took a break before continuing: "As far as the bake sale and the doggie treats are concerned, you're going to have to ask Joan. That's up to her. Let's discuss this more later. Right now I have to go paint Miss Nina's nails. I'll talk to her about this plan too—I know she's very involved in the shelter."

Mom headed back into the main salon.

The girls were speechless. That was the quickest Mom had ever agreed to *anything*. Aly didn't even have to make a list! And Mom wanted True Colors to get involved too! And be in the newspaper! And put posters up all over town!

They'd have to check with Paws for Love and get two "paws-up"—but once they did, the old-timers would be on their way to new homes. Or at least Aly hoped they would.

five

Reddy or Not

On Thursday night boxes of green- and red-pepper pizza were on the welcome desk. Lemonade and apple juice cartons sat on the windowsill. People sat in pedicure chairs, at manicure stations, some even on the floor. True Colors had never looked quite this way before.

It was the first meeting of the polish-a-thon planning committee, and the salon was packed. All the manicurists from True Colors were there, along with the Auden Elementary soccer team. Charlotte, Lily,

Sophie, and even Mrs. Franklin showed up. She'd left Sadie at home.

Joan and Aly were the "captains," while Mrs. Tanner was on the phone being interviewed by the local paper, *The Auden Herald*.

"It's great having you all here," Joan said. "We have a lot to figure out tonight. Anyone who wants to bake or be involved with selling the cookies and brownies and dog treats, come with me. Anyone who's going to help out with the polishing, you can talk to Aly."

Aly walked to the front door, a clipboard in her hands. Brooke, Lily, Sophie, Jenica, Mia, Giovanna, Joelle, Anjuli, and almost all the manicurists from True Colors followed. She was kind of nervous, looking at the group in front of her.

"First, thank you, everyone, for volunteering your time," she said quietly. Joan had helped her make a list of what to say, and it started with saying thank you.

"Speak louder!" Jenica said.

Aly turned bright red.

"I'm happy to do whatever it takes to get the dogs adopted," Jenica added.

"Me too," Mia agreed.

"Second, we have to go over the rules. Grown-up manicurists, an adult manicure is ten dollars. Sparkle Spa manicures are five dollars. If too many kids show up, we might have to send them to True Colors, since it's just Brooke and me polishing. My mom said that's okay—their manicures will still be five dollars."

Lisa, one of the salon's manicurists, nodded. "Sounds good," she said.

Aly smiled. She felt a bit more relaxed. "For the polish-a-thon, people can get only one color—not fancy stuff."

"That's too bad," Joelle said.

"It would take too long," Brooke told her, answering for Aly. "We have to go as fast as we can to raise enough money for all the puppies."

"What about featuring one special manicure for the day, an easy one—like a sparkle top coat or a rhinestoned pinkie?" Giovanna suggested.

Aly thought about that. If it was something easy, they could probably pull it off. Plus, people might be disappointed with just regular polish.

"A paw print!" Brooke said excitedly. "We could do a paw print on people's thumbs!"

"In a different color," Sophie added.

Aly nodded her head. "Okay, we'll do special paw print manicures and pedicures for anyone who wants them. I like it."

"It makes sense because of the dogs," Jenica said. "But what do we do? The people who aren't polishing?"

"You'll be assisting," Aly said. "The kind of stuff Brooke and I do for True Colors all the time."

"Like keeping the polish wall organized?" Joelle asked.

"Exactly," Aly said. "Joelle, do you want to be in charge of the polish display in the Sparkle Spa, and, Mia, you can be in charge of the wall in True Colors?"

Mia nodded.

Brooke's friend Sophie raised her hand. "I want a job," she said.

"We really need a polish checker, Sophie— someone who can make sure the bottles don't run too low and can replace them when they do. We also need someone to collect the donations."

"I can do that," Jenica said. "I'll do it in the main salon."

"And I'll do it in the Sparkle Spa," Lily said. "That's an easy job."

Aly wrote down everyone's roles. She said, "We also need two general helpers to empty trash cans, stack magazines, get customers coffee and water, and keep the jewelry station in the Sparkle Spa stocked with supplies."

"I'll do it for the Sparkle Spa," Anjuli said.

"And I'll do it in True Colors," Giovanna added.

Then she, Jenica, and Mia did a three-way high five. "Go Team True Colors!" Jenica cheered. "We'll make sure things run really smoothly," she assured the manicurists.

Lisa and Jamie smiled at her. Then Jamie turned to Aly. "Do you need us for anything else? We know the prices, we know the rules, and we know who's going to be helping us out."

Aly scanned the list on her clipboard. "I think that's it," she said. "Except—don't forget to get here extra, extra early on Sunday. The polish-a-thon starts at nine a.m. on the dot. Thanks again, everyone."

Aly glanced over at Joan's group. It looked like they, too, were wrapping up their discussion.

"Is it time for posters yet, Aly?" Brooke asked. Aly was amazed at how patient Brooke had been, quietly waiting.

Aly nodded. "Yep. Grown-ups can go grab some pizza. Girls, it's time to make some posters."

Brooke stood up and announced loudly, "Listen everyone. We need to make a ton of posters to hang all over town. I've got lots of markers and paper in the Sparkle Spa. You can draw wherever you want. I like the floor best."

Everyone pitched in, even Mom, who was an awesome artist. She drew pictures of puppies—some on posters, but some on smaller flyers, too, so she could photocopy them and hand them out around town.

Above, below, and all around the drawings, Aly

and some of the other girls filled in the space with all kinds of banners:

POLISH-A-THON FUND-RAISER FOR PAWS FOR LOVE ADOPTION DAY!

#5 Manicures for Kids!
#10 Manicures for Adults!

Baked Treats for Humans & Dogs: $2/each!

THIS SUNDAY, 9:00 A.M.-2:00 P.M.
AT TRUE COLORS NAIL SALON
ON MAIN STREET.

Then Brooke told the rest of the helpers to use real polish to color in the dogs' nails on the posters—she'd picked Reddy or Not. Aly thought the posters looked fantastic, especially Mom's. She had even drawn a dog that looked kind of like Sparky!

✳ ✳ ✳ ✳ ✳ ✳

Later that night Aly was brushing out Brooke's hair and weaving it into a French braid. It was the best way to sleep when you had long hair, Brooke had decided. That way, it didn't get too knotted up, and she didn't have a hard ponytail holder pushing into her head when she rolled over in her sleep.

"I can't believe the polish-a-thon is only three days away," Brooke said as Aly's fingers danced through her hair, making a neat and even braid.

"I know. It's fast," Aly said. She sometimes wondered if they should add French braiding to the services they offered at the Sparkle Spa. "But Adoption Day is a week from Sunday, and we need to make sure we have time to buy all the bows and sweaters and collars and bandanas and—"

"And paw-lish!" Brooke said, turning her head so fast that the braid slipped out of Aly's hands. "Don't forget the pet-icures."

Aly *had* almost forgotten the pet-icures. With all the polish-a-thon planning, she wasn't even thinking about next weekend.

"Are you worried about doing them?" Aly asked.

Brooke shook her head, and her braid started unraveling. "Nope. I think they're going to be the best part. I'm going to make Melvin look so nice that Mom's going to let us adopt him."

Ugh. Dumb, drooly Melvin. "Mom is never going to let us adopt Melvin," Aly said. "If she lets us adopt any dog, it would be Sparky. Sparky is the absolute cutest. Plus, he's little and doesn't drool all over everything."

"Melvin can't help it if he drools!" Brooke said. "That's so mean of you not to like him just because he drools. Would you hate *me* if I drooled?"

Aly could not believe they were having this argument. "Of course not," she said. "You're my sister. I'd love you no matter what. Even if you drooled every-where. And besides, it's not just the drooling. Melvin is huge."

"Would you hate me if *I* were huge?" Brooke asked, crossing her arms over her chest.

"Brooke!" Aly couldn't help yelling a little. "What I think about you is different from what I think about a big, drooly dog!"

Brooke's voice grew louder and louder. "I'm going to make sure that Melvin gets the best sweater and the best collar and the best pet-icure of all the old-timers. And then Mom and Dad will love him, and it won't even matter what you think."

"Just you wait." Aly could not stand the idea of Melvin being the best-looking dog on Adoption Day. "I'm going to make sure Sparky is the handsomest dog there. And Mom and Dad will love *him*, and then Melvin will go home with another family."

Brooke stood up. "Take that back!"

"I will not," Aly said, getting up herself and grabbing her pajamas out of her dresser.

Brooke stormed across the room to her own dresser and took out her pajamas, too. "And one more thing," she said, pushing her now-unraveled hair back over her shoulder. "You did the worst braid tonight. It already fell out." She started crying.

Aly couldn't believe it. Brooke had turned her head before Aly had been able to put an elastic at the bottom. She marched over to where she'd left Brooke's brush on the floor and threw it on Brooke's bed. "Maybe you should brush your hair yourself from now on."

Brooke glared at her. "Okay!" she shouted. "I will."

Aly climbed into bed and grabbed a book off her night table. At times like these, she wished she had her own room.

Six
Golden Delicious

For the next two days Brooke and Aly spoke to each other only when they had to discuss the polish-a-thon. They each led different teams of friends around to hang up posters in town, and even though they still had to share their bedroom, Brooke brushed her own hair and did her own braid at night. It wasn't as good as the ones Aly did for her, but at least it kept her hair out of her face when she slept.

Before the girls knew it, it was Sunday morning. Mom marched into their bedroom, pulled up the shades, and announced, "Happy Polish-a-Thon Day! Rise and shine!"

Aly rubbed the sleep out of her eyes. "Happy Polish-a-Thon Day," she grumbled.

"I just got an e-mail saying that the *Auden Herald* is sending a reporter to the salon today, and the local TV channel might even have cameras there. This is going to be great for business. Thanks for coming up with this idea, girls."

"TV!" Brooke said, jumping out of bed, her hair flying behind her. "We're going to be on TV?"

"Maybe," Mom said. "It's not definite."

But Brooke didn't seem to be listening anymore. "I'm going to wear a dress! The one with the ruffled skirt that's the same color as Magical Mystery Tour. And maybe Aly can fishbone-braid—" Brooke looked at her sister. "Never mind. I'll just wear it in one long ponytail."

Aly thought about offering to braid Brooke's hair for the polish-a-thon, but then she changed her mind. Brooke still hadn't apologized. Aly hadn't apologized either, but Brooke was the one who had started the Melvin vs. Sparky fight.

As Brooke got dressed, Aly pulled on her favorite long purple T-shirt and paired it with green leggings and high-tops.

Then both girls grabbed a piece of cinnamon toast their dad had made them, kissed him good-bye, and jumped into the car.

From the moment they got to the salon, every-thing was crazy!

"Girls!" Joan said. "I need help setting up the bake sale!"

"What do you need us to do?" Aly asked.

Joan handed one tray of bone-shaped dog treats to Aly and one tray of puppy-faced treats to Brooke.

The girls took them to Maxie and Bethany, who were waiting outside.

"These are for you," Aly said, putting her tray in the center of the table.

"Awesome. Joan told us that even though these are for dogs, they're safe for people to eat too," Bethany said. "I kind of wonder what they taste like."

"I'll try!" Brooke said. She picked up a bone-shaped treat and took a bite.

"Ew!" Maxie said. "I can't believe you ate that!"

Brooke shrugged. "It tastes kind of like peanut butter and oatmeal."

"Brooke! Aly!" Mom yelled out the door of the salon. "I need you!"

Aly and Brooke had been at True Colors for Perfectly Peach weddings, Silver Celebration birthday parties, and Sunday Pizza Picnics. But nothing could have prepared them for the polish-a-thon.

At nine o'clock, people started streaming in, and they didn't stop.

At eleven, the TV cameras and the newspaper showed up.

At noon, after Aly and Brooke had already done six manicures and two pedicures, Charlotte came in with her twin brother, Caleb.

"They're giving me a break from the bake sale table, so I'm here for a manicure," Charlotte said. "And Caleb, too! I told him it was okay for boys."

"No polish," Caleb said. "But Charlotte said you could get all the dirt out from under my nails. And, well, whatever. I like dogs."

Charlotte gave Lily a ten-dollar bill. "That's for both of us," she said.

"Thanks," Lily answered. "You can choose your color. And you can choose a separate color if you want a paw print on your thumb."

"A paw print—that's so cool." Charlotte smiled.

As soon as they finished one customer, another would sit down. The girls barely had a moment to breathe. Just when Aly thought it couldn't get any busier, a girl from Brooke's class named Tuesday came in.

She was carrying a rabbit! "Can you polish Fluffy's nails?" she asked. Then she looked around. "I thought this was for *animals*. On the posters the dogs were wearing polish."

As the Sparkle Spa's general helper, Anjuli should have handled this, but she was too busy talking to people in the waiting area. So Aly stopped her manicure and went over to talk to Tuesday.

"You'll have to take your rabbit home. But you can come back later or even another day to get your nails done. Okay?" Aly explained.

Disaster averted, Aly thought. But two more third

graders arrived with pets—a dog and a cat. Then a girl with a hamster showed up. And another one with a guinea pig.

Aly pulled Brooke behind the closet door. "What's going on?" she said. "Why are all these third graders coming with pets?"

Brooke's eyes started to get watery. "Maybe it's because I told them that we polished Sadie's paws."

"Did you tell them that we would polish their pets' paws too?" Aly hissed.

"Maybe," Brooke said, a tear rolling down her cheek. "I'm really sorry!"

Aly took a deep breath. She stood on a chair and made an announcement: "We can't do your pets' nails. You'll have to take them home. Please come back later or another day."

The girl with the hamster said, "But, Brooke, I thought you said—"

"I'm sorry," Aly said, still standing on her chair. "This polish-a-thon is for people only!"

The kids paraded out with their pets, and Aly and Brooke got back to three girls waiting.

"Next customer, please," Aly said. Then she turned to her sister. "Only fifteen more minutes, Brooke. Let's do these last ones quickly."

When two o'clock came and the last customer had left the salon, everyone cheered. Both True Colors and Sparkle Spa were total and complete messes: Bottles of polish, packages of nail files, stacks of washcloths, and piles of magazines covered every surface.

Aly took Charlotte's hand and said, "Come on, let's go outside just for a sec."

They sat on the Blue Skies bench in front of the store. Aly looked down at her hands, which were covered in what looked like a million shades of

Raspberry Rainbow, Cocoa Cupcake, and Cheer Up Buttercup.

Charlotte said, "Let's play Good, Better, Best. We haven't done that in forever!"

Aly grinned at her best friend. They had made the game up in third grade. It *did* seem like forever since the last time they had played.

Charlotte began. "Good was watching Joan do two manicures at once. Better was when Caleb stepped in that rabbit's poop. And best was . . ." She paused. "Best was having the reporter ask me about Paws for Love and me maybe being on TV. Your turn."

Aly thought for a moment and then said, "Good was that tons of people now know about Sparkle Spa. Better was watching Brooke eat about five of Joan's doggie treats. Yuck! And best was the best of all— making more than one thousand four hundred dollars for the puppies!"

seven
Hound Dog Blues

Immediately after school on Wednesday, Aly and Brooke raced to True Colors, picked up the polish-a-thon and bake sale money, and headed straight to Pups 'n' Stuff, the pet store where Miss Nina worked. It was one block plus two stores away from True Colors.

"How much did we make again?" Brooke asked, tugging on her braid, which Brooke did whenever she was nervous or excited. Aly knew that this time, it was because she was excited.

"One thousand four hundred and fifty-six dollars," Aly said, holding on to the pouch tightly. All the money wasn't in there, but a lot of it was. Mom had already given most of it to Mrs. Franklin so that the shelter could pay for baths and special groomers for all ten of the old-timers. They'd raised so much money, in fact, that the shelter was going to offer a free year's worth of dog food to any family who adopted one of the dogs on Sunday. "And we have six hundred and fifty-six dollars to spend on collars and sweaters and bows and bandanas and stuff."

Brooke nodded. "That's, um, six, um . . . how much money is that for each dog?"

Aly did the math in her head: *Six hundred and fifty-six divided by ten* . . . "Sixty-five dollars and sixty cents each. But it doesn't have to be exactly even." She thought maybe they could spend more money on Sparky and less on slobbery Melvin.

Brooke, of course, had other ideas. "You mean we can spend more on Melvin? I want to get him the best sweater in the store!"

Aly bit her tongue—hard enough that it even hurt a little. Both sisters seemed to have moved past the Melvin vs. Sparky fight, and Aly really didn't want to get into another one.

"Maybe," she said, stopping right in front of Pups 'n' Stuff.

Miss Nina was standing behind the counter as they walked in.

"Are you girls ready for Doggie Makeover Day on Saturday?" she asked. "My friends and I are going to bathe and groom all ten of the pooches."

Aly wasn't sure they were completely ready. Ten sets of four dog paws each was an awful lot of puppy nails to paint, even with their friends helping.

"I'm *so* ready!" Brooke said. "And we're here to

buy collars and bows and sweaters and bandanas and jackets."

"And paw-lish," Aly added. They couldn't forget that.

"Why don't we pick out the paw-lish first?" Miss Nina said, pushing up her sleeves.

She walked the girls over to the paw-lish bin and pulled out a few colors. "We have Bone White, Red Rover, Grass Green, Purple Paws, and Hound Dog Blues," she said.

"I think we need two of each," Aly said.

"Maybe not white," Brooke said. "That one's so boring."

"I thought maybe some of the boys could get white," Aly answered, picking up a tube of paw-lish. "You know, just in case red or purple doesn't go with their fur or their sweater or something."

Brooke scratched her head. "I think the boy dogs

won't mind. There are boys in my class who like red and purple."

Aly thought about that. Brooke was actually right—there were boys in her class who liked red and purple too.

"So just the four colors?" Miss Nina said.

Aly nodded.

"You know," Miss Nina added as she placed the paw-lish tubes on the counter, "my boyfriend wears nail polish. He's a rock musician. Lots of guys who play rock music wear nail polish."

"Maybe our dogs will be rock stars! Maybe *Melvin* will be a rock star!" Brooke said. She was looking at the different outfits and pulled out a leather vest. "This looks like Melvin," she said, bringing it to the counter.

Aly picked it up. It was pretty cool. But it was also $175. "Brooke," she said, "this is a little too expensive.

If we get him this, we won't have enough money to spend on the other dogs."

Brooke crossed her arms in front of her. "It's just because you hate Melvin. If you loved him like I did, you would get this vest. If it were for Sparky, you'd get it."

Aly sighed. "It's not that, Brooke. I don't hate Melvin. I just want to give all the dogs a fair chance. They all have to look good so they'll all get adopted."

Miss Nina walked over to a different wall and pulled down a black vest decorated with sparkly gold lightning bolts. "Here," she said, giving it to Brooke. "I think this will look neat on Melvin, just like a rock star. And it's much less expensive."

Brooke gave Aly one last glare and then inspected the vest. "Well, it *is* cool," she said.

"My boyfriend would love it." Miss Nina grabbed

a sparkly gold collar and leash, too. "And I think these match perfectly."

Brooke's face lit up. "Let's get those," she chirped.

Aly let out a big breath. At least Melvin was taken care of.

The girls split up the rest of the list, and with Miss Nina's help, they picked outfits for each dog.

For Bob, the one Charlotte liked: a plaid sweater with a green collar and leash.

For Marjorie: a pink T-shirt with a silver heart on the back, a silver collar and leash, and pink bows for her ears.

For Laces: a denim vest, a yellow collar and leash, and a yellow bandana for her neck.

For Reginald: a neon-green T-shirt with a fluorescent yellow leash and collar.

For Penny: a gold-and-silver-striped sweater, a silver leash and collar, and one gold bow.

For Frida: a dark-purple beret, a plum-colored bow, and a lavender collar and leash.

For Murphy: a black T-shirt with a silver star on the back and a matching silver leash and collar.

For Sneaker: a hot-pink warm-up jacket, a rhinestone collar and leash, and a hot-pink bow.

Slowly but surely, the pile on the counter got taller until only one dog was left: Sparky. What would make Sparky look his very best?

Aly looked at the clothing racks and shelves, and then she saw it: a little blue T-shirt with a sparkly rainbow on the back and a sparkly rainbow-colored collar and leash to match. He'd look like a walking version of their rainbow sparkle pedicure, and considering how magical that pedicure was for the soccer players, Aly figured it would be even more magical if it was all over Sparky's body.

Miss Nina rang up all the puppy outfits. "Six hundred and twenty-five dollars."

The girls were shocked—the clothing was so tiny; how could it cost so much?

"We have more than that," Brooke told her.

Aly unzipped the pouch and counted out the money, handing Miss Nina the exact amount.

"How much do we have left?" Brooke asked.

"Thirty-one dollars," Aly answered, and then she saw Brooke's eyes move around the store and zero in on a sign: FOR SALE: PUPPY PERFUME! $30!

Brooke made a beeline for the display. "This!" she said. "We need this so that they all smell good!"

She brought the bottle to Aly. Aly spritzed it in the air and sniffed. It smelled like fresh grass and clean laundry. Not bad. And they did have some money left.

"Okay," she said, handing Miss Nina another thirty dollars. "We can put this last dollar in the donation jar back at the Sparkle Spa," she told Brooke. "For whatever charity we decide to donate to next."

"It was so nice of you to raise the money for these dogs. There are so many dogs that need to be adopted and not enough people who get involved," Miss Nina said.

Aly watched Miss Nina's fingers as she started bagging all their merchandise and noticed the cool polish job. She felt kind of proud that it was her mom who did Miss Nina's manicure and applied the rhinestones to her pinkies.

"Did you two ever think about adopting a dog?" she asked.

"I looooove Melvin," Brooke said, pulling on her braid with one hand and holding one of the clothing bags with the other.

Aly picked up the second bag. "I like Sparky," Aly said. "But we're not allowed to have a dog. Our parents said."

Miss Nina nodded sympathetically. "Well, maybe you can get them to reconsider."

"I doubt it," Aly said. "They seem pretty serious about it."

As Brooke and Aly walked back to the salon, Aly thought it would be hard enough convincing her parents to adopt one dog. But two? No way. Especially if one of them was Melvin.

eight

Grass Green

All week long Aly had been thinking about Doggie Makeover Day. She hoped the old-timers would like their outfits and wouldn't squirm or chew or cry once they were dressed. She hoped all the groomers would show up. She hoped the pet-icures would go well.

She also hoped, deep down in the bottom of her heart, that somehow, magically, Mom and Dad would fall in love with Sparky and let her adopt him. And that bottom-of-her-heart hope was what

Aly was thinking about when she and Brooke were in the backseat of their dad's car on the way to the shelter on Saturday morning, with their bags of outfits and paw-lish and puppy perfume for the makeover event.

"You know, I had a dog when I was growing up," Dad told them from the front seat. "His name was Mouse, because he was huge. A sheepdog."

"That doesn't make sense, Daddy," Brooke said. "If he was so big, you should've named him Elephant or something."

"It was a joke, Brookie," Dad said. "Anyway, he was a great dog. If I were home more to help take care of it, I'd get you girls a dog, but it doesn't seem fair to leave all that work to your mother."

Aly thought about this for a moment. Was this good news in terms of possibly getting Sparky, or bad news? She wasn't quite sure.

"What was the best part about having a dog?" Brooke asked.

"Oh, I don't know if I could pick one thing," Dad said. "Dogs are good company, and they're fun to play with in the yard, and once Mouse even scared away a burglar."

"A burglar?" Brooke gasped. "Really, Daddy?"

"Yes. He was a special dog," Dad said, pulling up in front of the shelter. "You know, I'm proud of you girls for helping out the community like this, even though we're not getting a dog."

"Thanks, Dad," Aly said, her heart dropping into her stomach.

"Yeah, thanks," Brooke said, looking just as sad as Aly felt.

When the girls got out of the car, Mrs. Franklin and Sadie were waiting for them just inside the door—

dressed, as usual, like twins: Sadie wore yellow and pink bows on her ears. Mrs. Franklin had on a yellow-and-pink-striped hat.

"I'm so glad you're here," Mrs. Franklin said. "Your friends are already inside."

Charlotte, Lily, and Sophie were planning to help. And Jenica was going to be around, volunteering.

Aly and Brooke followed Mrs. Franklin through the shelter and waved at Irena, who was in the middle of a cat adoption. They finally reached the old-timers' room. "I'll be right back, girls," Mrs. Franklin said as she headed back down the hallway. "I have to let Isaac know you're here."

Miss Nina was already in the room, with Bob walking behind her on a leash. Lily, Sophie, and Charlotte were there too.

"Oooh, he looks so fluffy!" Charlotte squealed, kneeling down next to Bob. Miss Nina handed her

Bob's leash and went to get Marjorie out of her cage.

"Hi, Bob," Charlotte said. "Do you like it when people call you Bobby?"

Bob licked Charlotte's hand, and she laughed.

"Are you going to adopt him tomorrow?" Aly asked, putting her bag of dog accessories on the floor.

"I think so," Charlotte said. "My dad wants us to come here with Minerva to make sure they like each other. If they do, Bob's coming home with me."

"I'm getting Melvin," Brooke said.

Aly closed her eyes and started counting Mississippis so she wouldn't scream at her sister. "Stop it, Brooke," she whispered.

"The slobbery one?" Lily asked. "Ick. I didn't think anyone was going to take him. Are you sure that's the one you want?"

"We're not getting a dog," Aly said. "Brooke's just pretending. Right, Brooke?"

Brooke looked like she was about to cry. "I guess." She frowned.

"I'd pretend to get Sparky," Sophie said. "He's so cute, with those comic-book eyes. But I'm not allowed to have another pet—just my gerbil."

"I'd pretend to get Sparky too," Aly said. Then she walked over to his cage. "Hey, where is he?"

"He's in the back, waiting for his bath," Sophie said. "Miss Nina and the other groomers just started. They've got Bob, Laces, and Murphy done. And Marjorie's back there now, along with Frida and Sparky."

Bob started barking when Irena walked into the room with Isaac, Mrs. Franklin, and Sadie.

"Let's set you up in that corner over there," Irena said. "Isaac's going to be taking pictures. And don't worry if things get a little messy with the dogs."

Aly looked down at her T-shirt and jeans. She was glad she wasn't wearing any of her favorite clothes.

Irena continued, "There are towels and treats for the dogs, and a basket for all your dog polish."

"It's called paw-lish," Brooke told her. "And Hound Dog Blues is going to be the doggy Color of the Week." She giggled. "I mean, the Color of the Day."

Irena laughed. "Excuse me," she said. "Paw-lish. Anyway, I'll be coming in and out, but Nina said she'll keep an eye on you and the dogs. Isaac will be here too, if you need anything."

"Okay," Aly said, glancing up at Isaac. He smiled and gave her a thumbs-up.

"And," Irena said, leaning against one of the empty cages, "on behalf of the whole shelter: Thank you."

The girls polished the old-timers' nails, and the pups were yappy and didn't know if they wanted to sit, stand, or—in the case of Laces—roll over. But for the most part, they liked the attention and the treats, which Joan had made just for today and Aly had brought with her to the shelter.

As Aly was putting the finishing touches of Red Rover on Marjorie's back paw, she heard "Ew!" from the other side of the room, and "Ack!" She turned her head to see Lily holding her left hand with her right one. "I think Melvin tried to bite me!" she said. "I got my hand away in time, but that's so not cool."

Charlotte went racing to Lily. "Are you sure you're okay?" she asked, taking Lily's left hand in her own.

"Let me see," Miss Nina said, running at Charlotte's heels. She bent down and took Lily's hand from Charlotte. "No broken skin. Not even a mark," she said. "I think he was just trying to give you a kiss. He's a licker, not a biter."

"Well, I don't want to take him out of his cage," Lily said. "Either way, he's kind of gross."

Charlotte looked at the drool hanging down from his lips. "I don't think I want to either."

Brooke was tugging on her braid, clearly worried. She asked, "Can we polish Melvin's nails last? When all the other dogs are done?"

"Good idea, Brooke," said Miss Nina. "Let's finish up the others and then tackle Melvin."

Just then Jenica brought Sparky in from the back. "Hey, guys," she said. "One of the groomers asked if I could deliver this furball to you. He's such a sweetheart. I hope he goes to a great home."

Aly felt her heart tug. She hoped whoever got Sparky would love him as much as she would if he were her dog.

They had picked Purple Paws for Sparky, which went nicely with his rainbow collar and leash. But as cute and cuddly as Sparky looked . . .

He absolutely *hated* getting his pet-icure.

"Please don't take any pictures, Isaac," Aly pleaded. "I think the camera is making Sparky more nervous." Even though Aly was holding him steady, he shivered, whimpered, cried . . . and then peed on the floor.

"Yuck! It that what I think it is?" Lily squealed. The girls moved to the opposite side of the room, away from Aly and Sparky.

Luckily, Irena had come back into the room and took charge. "No worries. I'll take Sparky to the back and clean him up. But I don't think he's a candidate for nail polish," she said, and whisked him away.

Aly felt terrible. Without a pet-icure and with all his shivering, would anyone want Sparky?

She didn't have more than a second to worry, because it was finally time to do Melvin's paws. Miss Nina went to get him, since no one else would.

"He's so slobbery," Sophie said quietly. "I hope he doesn't bite anyone."

Aly knew Melvin was slobbery, but she was pretty sure he wasn't dangerous. If Miss Nina said he was nice, then Aly trusted her. But she understood if the other girls didn't.

"Brooke?" she asked, sending her a Secret Sister Eye Message by raising one eyebrow twice: *Can we do this—just us?*

Brooke smiled at Aly. "Teamwork," she answered.

Aly looked up at the rest of the girls from where she was sitting on the floor. "If you guys don't want to do Melvin, Brooke and I can do him, with Miss Nina's help." She knew Melvin was important to Brooke. And the Melvin versus Sparky fight didn't seem to matter as much as making sure he got a great pet-icure.

"You really wouldn't mind?" Charlotte asked.

"Nope," Aly said. "It's totally okay."

"It's okay," Brooke said. "Aly and I can do it." She walked over to Aly and grabbed her hand. The sisters knew that as a team they could do almost anything. Other people helping made things easier, but as long as they had each other, Aly and Brooke would be fine.

Miss Nina rubbed Melvin's head. "He's a good guy, I promise," she said, giving him a treat.

Aly and Brooke got to work, and were done pretty quickly, even with his drool. But maybe Brooke tickled Melvin, because he dropped his treat out of his mouth and licked her cheek, slobbering all over her face, the drool dripping down her neck.

"Ewwww!" Brooke said, but she was laughing. "Melvin, that's gross! There's spit all over me!"

While Brooke cleaned herself up, Aly tidied the pet-icure area, then stepped back to take in all the dogs at once. With their baths and new haircuts and colorful paws and sparkly collars, they looked like the most adoptable bunch of dogs ever. And once they had their new outfits on tomorrow, they'd look even more spectacular.

Sparky may not have had Purple Paws paw-lish on, but he still looked super adorable. What was most important, Aly realized, was that they were nice dogs on the inside too, even Melvin.

"You know what?" Brooke said, walking over to Aly. She was still scrubbing her neck with antibacterial wipes that Miss Nina had found for her. "I think you're right about Sparky."

"What do you mean?" Aly asked.

"I think," Brooke said, "he's the best dog for us. Better than Melvin after all."

Aly turned to her sister to see if she was kidding, but Brooke looked one hundred percent serious. "You think so?" she asked.

"Actually, I more than think so," Brooke said. "I know so." She stopped wiping her face long enough to tug on her braid. "Do you think we can make a list to convince Mom and Dad to let us adopt him tomorrow?"

Aly walked over to Sparky. "Hi, buddy," she said to the dog. His little nub of a tail wagged like crazy. Very slowly, Aly put her hand out and touched the dog's head. He licked her. And then licked her again and again. Brooke came over and petted him too, and he started licking her fingers.

"I think," Aly said, "that we should definitely try."

nine

Red Rover

After Mom had tucked the girls into bed that night, Aly reached into the crack between her bed and the wall and pulled out a small pad, an astronaut pen her dad had brought her back from New York City, and a miniature flashlight.

"Brooke," Aly whispered, pointing the flashlight beam at her sister, "are you ready to make our dog list?"

Brooke sat up in her bed with a stuffed animal in each arm and nodded.

"Okay, let's go," Aly said.

It wasn't a very long list. . . .

Why We Should Be Allowed to Get a Dog

1. Sparky needs a home.
2. Sparky is well-behaved. He doesn't bite or drool.

(Aly left out the part about him peeing during the pet-icure.)

3. Dad had a dog named Mouse that saved the house from a burglar, and Sparky's bark could save us from a burglar one day.
4. Sparky is the perfect size to take anywhere, so when we go visit Grammy and Papa, he can come too.

Aly and Brooke hoped it would do the trick. Tomorrow was not only Adoption Day—hopefully, it would also be Sparky Day.

When the Tanners drove over to Paws for Love, Dad couldn't stop saying how proud he was of Aly and Brooke.

"Did I mention how terrific you are?" he said.

Brooke laughed. "You *did*, Dad. You did yesterday."

"But you can say it again," Aly added. "We don't mind."

"It's true, we don't." Brooke was looking at Aly and raising her eyebrows high. *Now?* she mouthed about the Sparky list.

Aly shook her head again. She really hoped Brooke didn't jump the gun on this one.

"I'm looking forward to seeing what you did with these dogs," Mom said. "I'm impressed you were able to polish ten sets of dogs' nails yesterday."

"Nine," Aly said, and grinned at her sister.

"It wasn't that hard," Brooke said. "They're like people, but with funnier-shaped nails. Plus, our friends were there to help."

Mrs. Franklin and Sadie were in the front of the shelter. Sadie was wearing her best sweater—gray, woven through with silver sparkle thread—and a silver bow in her hair. Mrs. Franklin was holding an armful of flyers.

"Hi, Sadie!" Brooke said, getting out of the car.

"Hi, Mrs. Franklin," Aly said. "Were any old-timers adopted yet?"

"Yes," she answered. "Your friend Charlotte is inside, completing the paperwork for Bob. And Marjorie went first thing this morning. Nina is thinking about adopting Melvin, but I don't know if she's decided for sure yet."

Brooke looked up from petting Sadie. "I think Melvin and Miss Nina would make a great family. Especially because her boyfriend is a rock star and so is Melvin."

Mrs. Franklin looked confused, but Aly laughed. "Come on," she said, holding her hand out to her sister. "Let's go check out how the rest of them look."

But the girls didn't get too far. Joan was in the lobby with her dog treats, which she had named Joan's Bones. Each bone-shaped cookie was wrapped in plastic with a sticker on the front.

"Those look so good," Aly said. "Like they belong in a store."

Brooke and Aly saw Charlotte and her family leaving with Bob. He looked fabulous in his plaid sweater and green collar. As the Cane family waited to get their free-year's-supply-of-dog-food coupon, Caleb came over to Aly.

"I have a question for you," he said.

"What is it?" she asked. What could he want to ask her?

"Um, if I came to your, um, your room at the back of where your mom works, do you think you could make my thumbnails match Bob's? I like the green. There's, um, something cool about it."

Aly was surprised. A boy had never asked her for a manicure before. At least not one with polish—for his thumbs. She shrugged. "I guess," she said.

"Um, cool," Caleb said. And then he went back to his family.

Brooke was looking at Aly with her hands on her hips. "Are we doing *boys* now?"

"We were never *not* doing boys. Just none of them wanted to come," Aly said.

"I don't know about boys," Brooke said.

"Hey, Brooke! Hey, Aly!" A little girl with a

butterfly clip in her hair came running over to the sisters. It was Heather Davis, Suzy Davis's little sister, whose birthday party had been the very first Sparkle Spa event, when the girls opened their salon. "We just got a dog!"

Suzy came into the room next, with Sneaker on a leash. She was the dog that Aly and Brooke had dressed like a sparkly athlete, in a hot-pink warm-up jacket and a rhinestone collar and leash, with a hot-pink bow in her hair. Her nails were painted Red Rover.

"Why haven't you adopted a dog yet?" Suzy asked Aly. "Is it because your parents won't let you? Like how they won't let you wear nail polish during the school week?" Suzy rolled her eyes.

Aly ignored Suzy's questions. All she said was, "I hope you like Sneaker."

But then she turned to her parents. "Mom! Dad!"

she said. "We have to go look at the dogs."

"We have to! Now!" Brooke added.

The Tanners made their way into the old-timers' room. There were so many people there, and so many of the dogs were out of their cages. Aly tried to get through to Sparky's cage, but first she and Brooke were stopped by Anjuli, the goalie from the soccer team, who was adopting the tiny Yorkie named Reginald, and then Mrs. Bass, a True Colors customer, who seemed to be considering adopting Murphy, the bulldog.

Mom started talking to Mrs. Bass.

"I'm going to die of slowness!" Brooke whispered to Aly.

But Aly was thinking that she might die of worry. All around her, dogs seemed to be getting adopted. Lucas, whom half the sixth-grade soccer team had a crush on, was playing with Laces, the big golden retriever. Heather Davis's friend Jayden and a girl in Aly's grade named Annie were petting Penny the poodle.

Aly started to feel a little panicky. What if Sparky had been adopted? What if someone was playing with him right now and thinking about taking him home? What if he already found another family, before Brooke and Aly got to make their case for the dog? Aly checked her pocket for the list, just to make sure it was still there.

"Let's hold hands and push through the crowd," Aly told her sister. "We need to see if Sparky's still here. And if he is, then we can show him to Mom and Dad."

Brooke looked at Aly with terror in her eyes. "Do you think he could be gone?"

Aly took a deep breath. "I don't know, Brookster. I just don't know."

But just before they could start pushing their way to Sparky's cage, Irena saw them.

"Girls," she called "I'm so glad you made it! Look at what you've done. All these dogs are going to have homes because of you and your friends."

Aly and Brooke smiled and thanked her, but Aly couldn't stop her leg from bouncing with impatience. They *had* to find Sparky.

"You know, I think this is a record. All the dogs but one have been spoken for, and it's not even noon yet," Irena said.

Aly felt her heart start to race. "All but one have been adopted?"

Irena nodded, the beads on her braids clicking. "Isn't that wonderful?"

Brooke grabbed Aly's hand and squeezed it hard.

Aly swallowed.

"Which one—" she started to say, but the words

got caught in her throat, so she tried again. "Which one is left?"

Irena looked down at her clipboard.

Aly held her breath. *Please don't be adopted, please don't be adopted, please don't be adopted*, she wished.

ten

Call Me Sparkly

L et's see," Irena said. "It looks like the only one left is . . . Sparky." She smiled at the girls. "Maybe he's just a little too small for most people. It's a shame, though, because he's such a sweet dog."

Aly let out her breath in a whoosh. Thank goodness.

"Wewanthim!" Brooke blurted out so fast that her words ran together. "Please don't let anyone take him. We want him."

"Oh!" Irena looked surprised. "I thought you girls weren't allowed to have a dog."

"Would we be able to see him?" Aly asked. "So we can show him to our parents?"

"Of course," Irena said. "I'll go get him myself, for our star fund-raisers."

Irena left, and Aly pulled the list out of her pocket. "Okay, Brooke," she said. "I'm going to go get Mom and Dad away from Mrs. Bass. You wait here and hold Sparky when Irena comes back. Got it?"

"Got it," Brooke answered.

Weaving through the crowd, Aly made her way over to her parents. Mom was still in deep conversation with Mrs. Bass, but Dad was kneeling on the floor, petting Murphy, while Mrs. Bass's sons filled out the adoption papers. Aly kneeled down next to him and gave Murphy a pat. He was a really sweet dog and hadn't minded at all when his nails were painted.

"Hey, Dad," Aly said. "Brooke and I want you to meet someone."

"Hey, Alligator," he said. "This guy looks great." He gave Murphy another scratch behind his ears. "Who do you want me to meet?"

"It's a surprise," Aly told him. "Come with me."

Dad followed, and Aly threaded through the crowd of people and dogs and cages back to where Brooke was standing. She was holding Sparky, who kept trying to lick her face. His rainbow collar shone.

"You want me to meet Brooke?" Dad asked.

Aly started laughing. "No, Dad! We want you to meet Sparky."

"That little guy? Is he actually a dog?" Dad was joking, but Brooke didn't like it.

"Of course he's a dog!" she said, and handed Sparky over to her father. Dad was so much bigger than the tiny dog that Sparky fit right in the crook of his elbow. Sparky wasn't anything like Dad's dog

Mouse, but when he turned his head and licked Dad's fingers, Dad smiled.

"He's really sweet," Dad said. "Was he your favorite?"

Aly nodded.

Brooke said, "Well, not at first, but at second, yeah. And now I love him the most."

Dad looked down at Sparky. "So is one of your friends adopting him?" he asked.

Brooke looked at Aly. Aly cleared her throat. "We thought maybe we could adopt him," she said.

"There you are, girls. I thought I'd lost you," Mom said, walking over to Aly and Brooke. Then she saw the dog in Dad's arms. "Who's that?" she asked.

"It's Sparky," Brooke said. "He's the last dog left that doesn't have a family."

Aly handed Mom her list. "These are all the reasons why we think he'd be the perfect dog for us," she said.

Mom looked at the paper, then stepped closer to Dad so he could read it too. "You girls must've been thinking about this for a while," she said.

Brooke pushed her glasses up on her nose. "We have. For a very long time. At first I wanted Melvin, but he's really slobbery and too big, and Aly knew all along that Sparky would be the best one."

"He really is, Mom," Aly added. "And we think he'd be a great puppy for our family."

Mom looked down at the paper in her hand again and started reading it over carefully.

"Hi, everyone," Joan said, walking over to the Tanners. "Guess what? I just sold out of all the Joan's Bones." She was smiling.

"That's great news," Mom said.

Brooke couldn't wait another second. "Mom! We want a dog," she said. "The one Dad's holding."

Mom gave Dad and Joan a look. "I'm not sure if our

house can handle a dog. And he'd be home alone all day. That's not a very nice way for a dog to spend his time."

Aly hadn't thought of that. That was a problem. She didn't want Sparky to be alone all day. There had to be a way to make this work. She had to think fast.

"How about the Sparkle Spa?" Aly said. "What if he lives at the Sparkle Spa during the day? We could get him a bed and toys, and he could live in the corner next to the pedicure chairs. We could even get him an enclosure gate so he won't be able to go into the main salon and wander around."

Mom tilted her head sideways. She raised her eyebrows at Dad. Brooke started bouncing on her toes.

"Who would walk him?" Mom said. "While you girls are at school?"

"Um . . . ," Aly began.

Joan raised her hand. "I could do it," she said.

"Really?" Brooke asked, throwing her arms around Joan. "You'd do that?"

"Sure," Joan answered. "I love dogs. It would be fun to have one at the salon."

Dad cleared his throat. "You girls have been so responsible with the fund-raiser and the shelter dogs, I bet you'd do a great job with Sparky. But you know I'm not around very much, so this decision is really up to your mom."

"I promise we'll take such good care of him," Aly said. "You won't have to do a thing!"

Brooke nodded. Then she took Sparky out of Dad's arms and handed him over to their mom.

Mom's face looked soft and sweet. The girls knew they had her—it was love at first sight. Or first cuddle.

"Well . . ." Mom looked at Joan again. "You're sure you want to take on the dog-walking responsibility?"

Joan ruffled Aly's hair. "Absolutely," she said.

"You girls *have* been very responsible," Mom said. "And since Joan is willing to help, I say okay."

Brooke screamed and threw her arms around Mom and Sparky. "Thank you, Mommy!" Then she hugged her dad.

But Aly turned and hugged Joan. "Thank *you*," she said quietly. "Mom never would've agreed otherwise."

"My pleasure," Joan said as she gave Aly a squeeze. Then Aly went to hug her parents, too. She was smiling so wide, her cheeks were hurting a bit, but she couldn't stop. Other than the day she and Brooke got Mom to agree to the Sparkle Spa, this was one of the happiest days of Aly's life.

When they had all the adoption papers signed and the coupon for a free year of dog food from Pups 'n' Stuff in hand, the Tanners—along with Joan and, of course, Sparky—walked over to True Colors. Dad had already taken the car and would meet up with them at the salon.

Aly was holding Sparky's leash, the sparkly rainbow one that she'd picked out herself, and Brooke was telling Sparky all about the salon.

"There's lots of nail polish there," she was saying, "but it's not the kind for you. You have special nail polish. This kind at the Sparkle Spa is just for people."

Sparky twitched his ears. Aly started laughing.

When they reached True Colors, Aly and Brooke sat outside on the Blue Skies bench. Aly held Sparky on her lap, and while she rubbed his belly, she couldn't help but come up with a good, better, and best for today:

Good was that she and Brooke were friends again, no matter what.

Better was that all the old-timers were adopted into loving homes.

And best was that the cutest old-timer of all was their brand-new dog.

Brooke interrupted her thoughts. "Aly? Let's take Sparky into the Sparkle Spa so he can see how cool it is." The sisters walked into True Colors and headed for the back room. They watched Sparky sniff around, getting to know his new home.

"Can you believe Mom really agreed?" Brooke asked.

Aly shook her head. "It's kind of a miracle."

"There's one thing," Brooke said.

"What's that?" Aly asked.

"I think we have to change his name."

"Change his name?" Aly asked. "Won't that be confusing for him?"

"Not change it *too* much," Brooke said. She was

over near the polish display, grabbing a bottle out of the silver section. "Here!" she said. She ran over and gave the polish to Aly.

"Call Me Sparkly," Aly read. "I forgot about this color."

"See?" Brooke said. "His name *should* be Sparkly."

Aly smiled. As usual, Brooke's ideas turned out perfectly in the end. Sparkly it would be.

How to Give Yourself (or a Friend!) a Puppy Paw Pedicure

By Aly (and Brooke!)

✳ ⋅⋅✳⋅⋅✳⋅⋅✳⋅⋅✳⋅⋅✳⋅⋅✳

What you need:

Paper towels

Polish remover

Cotton balls

Clear polish

One color polish for the base (we suggest yellow)

One color polish for the paw prints (we suggest pink)

Watercolor paintbrush

What you do:

1. Put some paper towels down on the floor so you don't have to worry about what will happen if you spill some polish. (Seriously. This is important. Polish stains badly. We know from experience.)

2. Take one cotton ball and put some polish remover on it. If you have polish on your toes already, use enough to get it off. If you don't, just rub the remover over your nails once to get off any dirt that might be on there. (If there's dirt, it'll make your polish look lumpy. And lumpy polish is the absolute pits!)

3. Rip off two paper towels. Twist the first one into a long tube and weave it back and forth between your toes to separate them a little bit more. Then do the same thing with the second paper towel for your other foot. You might need to tuck it in around your pinkie toe if it pops up and gets in your way while you polish.

4. Open up your clear polish, and do a coat of clear on each nail. Then close the clear bottle up tight. (You can go in whatever order you want, but our favorite is big toe to pinkie on your

right foot, then big toe to pinkie on your left foot. Just make sure you get them all!)

5. Open up the yellow polish. (Or whichever color you chose for your base. Just make sure it's a color that will make it so you can see the paw print! For example, orange on red might be a little hard to see.) Do a coat on each toe. Close the bottle up tight.

6. Fan your toes a little to dry them a tiny bit, and then repeat step five. (If you don't do a second coat, the polish won't look as beautiful and bright.)

7. Fan your toes again. (You should fan them for a while. We recommend singing the whole alphabet song three times through. Aly likes to show off and sing it backward, but I do forward and that's just fine.)

8. Open up your pink polish (or whatever accent color you chose). Don't use the regular polish brush. Take the watercolor paintbrush, which has thinner and pointier hairs, and dip it into the pink polish. Then touch the paintbrush to the middle of your big toenail to make a medium-sized dot. After that, touch it above the medium-sized dot three times to make three smaller dots in a row. It'll look just like a paw print! (If it doesn't, you can just get nail polish remover and start over.) Then do it on the other big toenail. (You could do it on every nail, but we think it looks cooler on the big toes. Also, the rest of the toenails are pretty tiny, so it's hard to make the dots small enough to make the paws.) When you're done, close the bottle up tight.

9. Fan your toes a little bit (one alphabet song should do the trick) and then open your clear

polish. Do a top coat of clear polish on all your toes. Close the bottle up tight.

10. Now your toes have to dry. You can fan them for a long time (like at least fifteen alphabet songs), or sit and make a bracelet or read a book or watch TV or talk to your friend. Usually it takes about twenty minutes, but it could take longer. (After twenty minutes, you should check the polish really carefully by touching your big toe super lightly with your thumb. If it still feels sticky, keep waiting! Patience is the most important part, otherwise you might smudge it and you'll have to take it off and do it all over again, which, let me tell you, is a very grumpy-making thing.)

And now you should have a beautiful puppy paw pedicure! Even after the polish is dry, you probably shouldn't wear socks and sneaker-type shoes for a while. Bare feet or sandals are better so all your hard work doesn't get smooshed. (And besides, then you can show people your puppy paw toes!)

Happy polishing!

✳ ✳ ✳ ✳ ✳ ✳